FLEABAG MONKEYFACE

The au_____ _____book to
the invento_____nd yellow
– withou_____ would

First published 2008 by Walker Books Ltd
87 Vauxhall Walk, London SE11 5HJ

2 4 6 8 10 9 7 5 3 1

© 2008 Duncan McCoshan and Jem Packer

The right of Duncan McCoshan and Jem Packer to be identified
as author/illustrator of this work has been asserted by them
in accordance with the Copyright, Designs and Patents Act 1988

This book has been typeset in Shinn Light

Printed and bound in Great Britain by Clays Ltd, St Ives plc

British Library Cataloguing in Publication Data:
a catalogue record for this book is available
from the British Library

ISBN 978-1-4063-1403-8

www.walker.co.uk

A NOTE FROM THE PUBLISHER

We apologize for what you are about to read!

You may find the images of fairies **cavorting**, ballet dancers **flouncing** and unicorns **prancing** make you want to lie down...

We suggest you keep copies of the first two Fleabag books handy in case you start to feel queasy. Because this story contains scenes of **extreme fluffiness**.

So don't tell us we didn't warn you!

But before we get to the horrible fluffy stuff, let's meet our heroes, **Gerald**, **Gene** and **Fleabag Monkeyface**. Here's a few things you need to know about them:

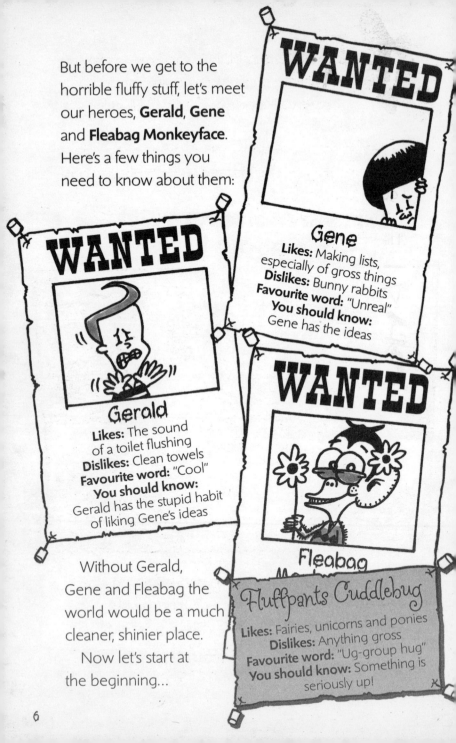

WANTED

Gene
Likes: Making lists, especially of gross things
Dislikes: Bunny rabbits
Favourite word: "Unreal"
You should know: Gene has the ideas

WANTED

Gerald
Likes: The sound of a toilet flushing
Dislikes: Clean towels
Favourite word: "Cool"
You should know: Gerald has the stupid habit of liking Gene's ideas

WANTED

Fleabag Monkeyface

Without Gerald, Gene and Fleabag the world would be a much cleaner, shinier place.

Now let's start at the beginning...

Fluffpants Cuddlebug
Likes: Fairies, unicorns and ponies
Dislikes: Anything gross
Favourite word: "Ug-group hug"
You should know: Something is seriously up!

1 It was Gerald's birthday and he was having a great time but something was missing.

"Where's Fleabag?" he said. "Still acting weird?"

"Afraid so." Gene sighed. "It's like he's not gross any more. But don't let that spoil your birthday. Look, I got you a present."

"I hope it's something EXTRA gross!" said Gerald. "I like the rotting banana skin wrapping paper."

Now most kids would like to get something nice, like a bicycle or a football, for their birthday. But Gerald, Gene and Fleabag weren't like most kids, and whenever one of them had a birthday, the others would try to get them the grossest gifts they could find.

"**Garbage Dump Dummies!**" marvelled Gerald, holding up three action figures. "These are too cool for words. Thanks, Gene!"

"They've only just hit the stores," said Gene. "In fact, I was the first person to buy them. They're going to be the next big craze, and we've got them first!"

Now you've probably seen action figures before – you may even have some in your bedroom right now – but you've never seen anything like the Garbage Dump Dummies. Let's take a closer look...

"I can't wait to show these to Fleabag!" said Gerald. "Their special powers are amazing!"

Just then Fleabag appeared ... carrying a large fruit bowl.

"Happy ug-birthday!" he said. "I ug-got you an ug-bowl of exotic fruity treats."

"Thanks, Fleabag, but these aren't even rotten," said Gerald. "Are you feeling all right?"

"No, I'm ug-not," said Fleabag, pointing at the Garbage Dump Dummies. "Those are ug-yucky! I ug-need some ug-fresh air. Ug-now!"

"Fresh air?" said Gene. "I thought Fleabag was allergic to fresh air."

But Gerald and Gene were too busy to think about Fleabag's new love of fruit and fresh air – they had brand-new action figures to check out!

2 The next morning Gerald and Gene were heading to school. (Fleabag had left early because he wanted to take his time and admire the clouds.) For once they were in a hurry to get there because it was Show and Tell Day.

"Did you pack everything?" said Gene.

"Stinky, check!" said Gerald. "Filthy, check! Dirt, check!"

"At last there's an alternative to those nauseating *Fluffy Bunch* characters!" said Gene.

"Fairies and unicorns – **yuck!**" said Gerald.

The Fluffy Bunch were the opposite of Garbage Dump Dummies but were still hugely popular (if not with Gerald and Gene).

You may find this unpleasant, but let's meet some of them...

Gerald and Gene couldn't wait to show everyone their Garbage Dump Dummies. Luckily they were up first in the Show and Tell.

"Welcome to the World of Garbage Dump Dummies!" said Gerald.

"Put those disgusting things away!" said
Mr Troutman, holding a hanky over his nose.
"Now I hope the next person has something
a little less revolting to show us."

"I ug-do," said Fleabag Monkeyface.

"This had better not be gross," warned Mr Troutman
as he opened a window.

Carefully placing his bag on a table, Fleabag gently
opened it and held up ... a fluffy pink pencil case.

"This is an ug-Blinky the Sparkliest Unicorn pencil
case," he said. "Inside I ug-keep a set of My Cuddly-
Wuddly Pony crayons, and look here's my ug-fave
Fabby the Fabby-Wabby Wee Fairy rubber – it plays
its own ug-tune! They're just an ug-few of my
ug-favourite Fluffy Bunch characters."

"What's going on with Fleabag?" whispered Gerald. "Normally he wouldn't even *touch* a Fluffy Bunch product, never mind own one!"

But things were about to get a lot worse...

"This term's school trip is a visit to a very special place," Mr Troutman said excitedly. "It's the trip of a lifetime for all Fluffy Bunch lovers – the class has been given tickets to *Fluffyland* theme park!"

The whole class cheered – well, everyone except Gerald and Gene. Fluffyland was the last place on earth any lovers of gross out would go because it was the Fluffy Bunch theme park. But to Gerald and Gene's horror, Fleabag was cheering the loudest!

YIPPEE-DIPPEE-DOODA!!!!

Eventually Mr Troutman calmed the class down and began the day's lesson.

"Today we will be looking at the siege of Troy, and how the Trojan horse was used to..."

But at the back of the room, Gerald and Gene were more concerned with Fleabag than Trojan horses.

"What's going on?" hissed Gene. "What's happened to the *old* Fleabag?"

THE FLEABAG WHO FOUGHT OFF EARMAGEDDON WITH HIS OWN EARWAX. *

THE FLEABAG WHO DEFEATED KING PONG WITH A TURBO-SNEEZE. **

THE FLEABAG WHO **LOVED** GROSS.OUT! ***

Filthy Footnotes
* See The Disgusting Adventures of Fleabag Monkeyface: When Earwax Attacks
** See The Disgusting Adventures of Fleabag Monkeyface: King Pong
*** See any Disgusting Adventures of Fleabag Monkeyface book

3 Over the next few weeks there was still no sign of the old Fleabag. In fact he was getting worse. He was spending more time on his own "re-decorating" his home, the **Gross-Out Den** (it was once an outside toilet!).

"What's going on in there?" said Gerald. The Gross-Out Den was hidden by large plastic sheets as frantic work and constant deliveries took place.

"I'm sure he's having a shower installed." Gene shuddered. "And that's the fifth delivery of pot plants today."

"All he talks about is the school trip to Fluffyland," added Gerald. "He says, he's 'so ug-excited' he can hardly 'ug-breathe'!"

Fortunately Gene had an idea that was sure to get the old Fleabag back. Gerald, Gene and Fleabag have their own TV show, **Gross-Out TV** – although their disgusting adventures always seem to get in the way of them actually making any programmes...

"I've got the perfect place to make a film!" said Gene. "We've received a special invitation."

"Really? Where are we going this time?" asked Gerald excitedly. "A nappy factory? The world's biggest compost heap?"

"Somewhere *much* grosser than that," said Gene. "We've been invited to a brand-new theme park – Garbage Dump Dummy World!"

As Gene had predicted Garbage Dump Dummies were catching on, and a huge theme park had just been built – one to rival Fluffyland.

"Cool!" said Gerald. "When do we go?"

"Tomorrow," said Gene. "We're going to be shown round by the inventor of Garbage Dump Dummies himself, Samuelson Stinx!"

"Let's hope the trip gets Fleabag back to normal," said Gerald. "We need our star presenter."

It took a lot of begging but Fleabag finally agreed to go after Gerald and Gene bribed him with a Blinky the Sparkliest Unicorn flashing horn.

4 The next day Gerald, Gene and Fleabag set out for Garbage Dump Dummy World, which was right next to Fluffyland. Gerald and Gene shuddered as they passed the fluffy theme park but Fleabag got very excited.

"Come on, Fleabag," said Gene. "You love gross out, remember?"

They finally persuaded him to move on and eventually arrived at the gates of Garbage Dump Dummy World. The door was a huge gaping mouth, and as it creaked open there was a loud belching noise and a green vapour sprayed into the air.

"Even the entrance is gross!" marvelled Gene.

Through the green mist they could make out a small figure: the Garbage Dump Dummies' creator himself, **Samuelson Stinx**!

"Welcome, welcome! It's great to have some real fans visiting!" he said, ushering them into his theme park. "When I neard you were the first kids to buy my action figures just had to get you along for a preview. Now follow me."

And everything was GROSS!

The snacks...

CABBAGE-FLAVOURED CANDYFLOSS. YUM!

The staff...

Even the souvenirs in the shops!

"This place is amazing!" said Gene, taking it all in.

"We love Garbage Dump Dummies!" said Gerald. "They're so much better than all those horrible Fluffy Bunch characters."

"Thank you," said Mr Stinx, before adding anxiously, "But I don't think the **Fluffy Bunch Corporation** is too happy about us opening up. I've had some pretty irate fairies checking the place out."

"Well, we know where *we'd* rather go," said Gene.

"Great!" Mr Stinx beamed. "Now let me show you the rides!"

If Gerald and Gene had loved the stalls and shops, then nothing had prepared them for the rides – pure adrenaline with a healthy dose of gross out thrown in... They had a go on **Filthy's Cheese Grater of Doom**.

They held on tight for **Dirt's Grotty Ghost Train**.

They screamed their heads off on the **Disgusto Plunge**.

And they begged for mercy on **Revolto's Roller Coaster.**

"Unreal!" said Gene as they finished the final ride.

"Cool!" said Gerald. "This place is great! Time to get filming..."

"I'm ready to roll. Fleabag get into position!" said Gene. But their star presenter was nowhere to be seen. Gerald and Gene had been having so much fun they hadn't noticed that Fleabag had vanished.

"I'm sorry, Mr Stinx, but we need to track down Fleabag," said Gerald. "He seems to have disappeared."

5 Gerald, Gene and Mr Stinx searched every corner of Garbage Dump Dummy World, but there was no sign of Fleabag.

"There is one last place we can try," said Mr Stinx. "My workshop – it's where I develop all my new ideas and products."

When they reached the huge building, the door was open.

"He must be in here," said Mr Stinx, leading them through his workshop. Half-built action figures, accessories and gross-out gadgets lay everywhere.

"How cool is this?" said Gerald as they walked past huge work benches of unfinished toys. "What are you working on now?"

"My latest gadget – **Gross-Out Goggles**," said Mr Stinx. "If you wear these everything appears gross. Here, try a pair."

Gerald and Gene both put on Gross-Out Goggles. At first everything seemed normal, then Mr Stinx held up a fairy cake.

"Wow!" said Gene. "It looks rotten!"

"And there's a huge worm in the middle of it!" said Gerald.

"Pretty amazing, eh?" said Mr Stinx. "I'm still field-testing them. Why don't you take a few pairs and let me know how you get on. Now, where is your monkey friend?"

Just then they heard squeaks of joy
coming from the back of the workshop.
And there was Fleabag – surrounded by
enormous fluffy creatures!

"This place is so much ug-better,"
he said, cuddling a huge bunny.

"What are these?!" asked
Gene, horrified.

"They are
prototypes
I was working
on for the
Fluffy Bunch
Corporation,"
said Mr Stinx.
"I'm customising
them to be gross.
I've already fitted
a belching
mechanism to
that bunny."

"You used
to work for the Fluffy Bunch
Corporation?"
said Gerald.

"Yes," confessed Mr Stinx. "But
I got sick of designing cute characters
and they fired me."

"Now I really must ask your furry friend to leave," he continued. "Some of these prototypes are unstable... If Fleabag sets off the belching mechanism in that bunny we'll all be toast."

But it was too late! Fleabag was cuddling the bunny so hard that there was a loud clicking noise.

"5 ... 4...!" boomed a robotic voice as the bunny lurched in their direction.

"There's no escape!" cried Gene. "We're hemmed in by giant ponies and unicorns!"

"Fleabag, use your **Gross-Out Power** or we're done for!" implored Gerald.

"3 ... 2..." continued the bunny.

"Oh no!" shrieked Mr Stinx.

Despite going Fluffy, Fleabag was not about to let his friends be blown away by a belching bunny and he jumped into action...

"Ug-dentist fresh menthol burp!" he cried, before emitting a clean fresh-smelling burp that shot him into the air. Fleabag's Gross-Out Powers had gone fluffy!

"... 1 ... BELCH OFF!!!" said the bunny, opening its mouth wide...

"Bionic ug-soap pellets!" said Fleabag, as a volley of teeny-weeny soaps shot out of his ear.

The bunny was pushed back, but it still looked determined to belch.

"Use a turbo-fart!" cried Gerald.

"Rear-end perfumed puffette!" said Fleabag, releasing an explosion of meadow-fresh aroma.

"Malfunction... Malfunction...!" stuttered the bunny as it tumbled back in a heap.

Fleabag's **Not-So-Gross-Out Power** had saved the day!

FFWFFT!

"That was close!" said Mr Stinx.

"I need to go ug-home. I feel ug-faint..." said Fleabag.

"Looks like filming is over for today," said Gerald. "Thanks, Mr Stinx, it was amazing!"

"Sorry about your bunny," said Gene. "And thanks for the Gross-Out Goggles – we'll let you know how we get on with them."

As they headed home Gerald and Gene decided it was time to find out what was going on with their hairy best friend.

"Those Fluff-Out Powers were the last straw," said Gene.

6 But more worrying developments were under way in Fluffyland. At the heart of the theme park sits *Fluffy Castle*, a pink fairy-tale palace surrounded by a pink moat with a pink sign.

WARNING!
Fluffy Bunch Corporation
Headquarters
Trespassers will be
tickled to death

Inside, Gwendolina, Fairy Queen and Head of the secretive Fluffy Bunch Corporation, was looking at brand-new characters. Although the Corporation had a whole host of fluffy characters, it was always on the lookout for the next big thing and Gwendolina's personal assistant, Fifinella the Fairy-tale Princess, was showing her the latest collection.

"These are going to be huge!" said Fifinella, trembling with excitement.

"I'll be the judge of that," snapped Gwendolina. "Show me what you've got!"

"First of all meet Hugsy the Huggable Hedgehog. We believe there's an untapped market in huggable characters. We're already working on the TV show.

"Then there's Twitty and Flitty and the Tweeniferous Family of Woodland Dwellers. A whole family of cute woodland folk – just think of the sticker album!

"Finally, my personal favourite, Minny-Twinkle the Marvellous Mermaid. A mini-mermaid – genius! The cuddly toy potential alone is massive!"

"Pathetic," hissed Gwendolina. "We've got all the magical, cuddly characters we need already!"

"Pathetic?" quivered Fifinella.

"Have you seen the theme park they've opened next door?" barked Gwendolina. "We're going to need more than mermaids and hedgehogs to take *them* on. Fortunately, *I've* got a plan."

"A plan?" queried Fifinella. "What kind of a plan?"

"You'll find out more at the **Emergency General Meeting**," snapped Gwendolina. "But the first part is already in place. I have recruited someone from the **Dirty Side**. One they call 'Fleabag Monkeyface'."

"The D-D-Dirty Side?!" whimpered Fifinella. "Fleabag Monkeyface? Even his name makes me feel ill."

"I know, but this 'Fleabag' has great powers," said Gwendolina. "Powers we will need for my plan."

"But how did you get Flea-whatever to join?" asked Fifinella. "By tickling? By polished polite persuasion?" "Far simpler than that," said Gwendolina. "By poison!"

"Fabby Fairy Flakes is our best-selling brand of cereal...

The one they call Fleabag would never eat these so I planted a box with a thirty-year-old sell-by date in his Gross-Out Den...

I knew he would soon tuck into the rotten old cereal, including the **Lucky Fabby Fairy Charm** that comes free in every box...

"As you can see, my deliciously devious plan is developing delightfully." Gwendolina beamed. "Now did you get what I ordered?"

"Yes, but we had a huge job tracking down a thousand puppy dogs," said Fifinella. "We normally only have a dozen or so for the Fluffy Games Puppy Pageant."

"And did you invite the monkey-one's school to Fluffyland?" asked the Fairy Queen.

"Yes, but couldn't we just get this Fleabag to come along?" said Fifinella.

"We need to avoid suspicion. By inviting the whole school to visit on the same day as the **Fluffy Games**, the biggest day of the fluffy sports calendar, no one will suspect a thing," said Gwendolina proudly. "Special Agents Randy and Mandy Smugley will escort Fleabag to the Games. Then everything will be in place to blow that lousy Garbage Dump Dummy World out of the water FOR EVER!!!"

7

Meanwhile, Gerald and Gene were
preparing to confront Fleabag.

"Look, he's changed the sign," said Gerald, as they
approached the newly decorated Gross-Out Den.

"Yuck!" spluttered Gerald. "And what's that smell?
It's disgusting."

"It's ... it's ... air freshener!" choked Gene. "And
what's with the weird paint job?"

"Flowers and all that pink! **Eugh!**" said Gerald.
"We've got to save him!"

"I don't remember a doorbell," he continued, pressing the button. In the distance they could hear the sound of birds tweeting. But birdie doorbells were nothing compared to what awaited them when the door opened.

"Ug-greetings," said Fleabag. "And ug-welcome to my new-look ug-humble abode."

The Gross-Out Den was unrecognizable. Gone were the cabinets that housed the Gross-Out Museum, gone were the piles of rotting food from Fleabag's kitchen and gone was the toilet Fleabag used as a bed. Instead everything was sparkly clean and there were Fluffy Bunch toys everywhere.

"Verily, I'm just ug-out of the ug-shower," said Fleabag. "Now can I ug-get you some ug-organic fairy ug-cakes?"

But before Gerald and Gene could quiz Fleabag they were interrupted by the doorbell tweeting again.

"OH NO, IT'S THE SMUGLEYS!" wailed Gerald and Gene.

Randy and **Mandy Smugley** along with their pets, **Lamby** and **Wamby**, were Gerald, Gene and Fleabag's arch-rivals and next-door neighbours. Lovers of all things clean and cute, they were the complete opposite of Gerald and Gene, but the new-look Fleabag actually seemed pleased to see them.

"**W**hat do you want?" said Gerald, hoping they would go away.

"And why have you got suitcases?" said Gene, pointing at their My Cuddly-Wuddly Pony luggage. "Going somewhere far away, I hope?"

"Our bags contain sports kit," replied Mandy. "We're in training and we're here to pick up our friend."

"Friend? In here?" said Gerald doubtfully. "I think you're in the wrong Gross-Out Den."

"Oh, I don't think so," said Randy Smugley, barging past Gerald and Gene. "This is **The Lovely Hut**, right? Oh, Fluffpants! Are you ready?"

Gerald and Gene almost collapsed as they witnessed one of the grossest sights they'd ever had the misfortune to lay their eyes on. The Smugleys and their pets were *hugging* Fleabag – and he seemed to be enjoying it!

"You give the best hugs, Fluffpants. Now I hope you're ready for a serious training session," said Mandy Smugley.

"Ug-ready to go!" Fleabag beamed.

"Whoa! whoa, time out!" said Gene. "Who exactly is Fluffpants?"

"That is ug-me," said Fleabag. "Fleabag Monkeyface is far too ug-gross a name. From now on I want to be ug-known as **Fluffpants Cuddlebug**!"

"But that name isn't gross at all," said Gerald. "How did you even think it up?"

"*We* thought it up," said Randy proudly. "'Fluffpants' because he's fluffy like a brand-new pair of pants."

"And 'cuddle' because he's cuddly like a kitten and 'bug' because he's cute like a ladybird," added Mandy. "Now we must be on our way!"

"But where are you taking Fleabag?" asked Gene. "And what is this 'training session'?"

46

"The name is ug-Fluffpants, and we're in ug-training for the ug-Fluffy Games!" said Fleabag proudly.

"The what?!" said Gerald.

"Let me explain," said Randy. "Every four years lovers of all things cute and cuddly gather in the courtyard of Fluffy Castle..."

The selected few get to compete for medals in events like Cardigan Folding...

New world records are set in events like Speed Flower Arranging...

Television cameras capture every minute of the Kitty Cuddle-thon – where you have to cuddle a kitten for twenty-six hours...

"But best of all, they get to watch the Puppy Pageant!" squealed Mandy.

47

"But only the Fluffiest are invited to compete," said Randy. "And we think with the right training Fluffpants might just qualify!"

Then without so much as an "ug-bye", Fluffpants and the Smugleys were off and hard at training in the Smugleys' garden.

But if Gerald and Gene thought that was bad, then what was happening just outside town would wobble them to the tips of their toes...

Deep within Fluffyland a long queue of strange-looking figures was entering Fluffy Castle. Some floated, some flew, some had four legs and some had wands.

THIS WAY, FLUFFY ONES!

WARNING!
The next pages contain scenes of extreme fluffiness.

"Greetings, Oh Fluffy Ones," said Gwendolina, who was sitting at the head of a huge table.

"Greetings, Gwendolina, Oh Super-Duper Sovereign of Sparkle!" responded the crowd.

"Thank you for coming to this Emergency General Meeting," she continued. "I have important news."

"The new range of Blinky the Sparkliest Unicorn baby rattles are out?" bleated an excited elf. "The ones that light up when a baby giggles?"

"You're here to show us the new My Cuddly-Wuddly Pony tea set," added a ballerina, clapping her hands. "The one with the twinkly-winkly teapot?"

"HUSH!" barked Gwendolina. "I have not gathered you here to talk about merchandise. I'm here to tell you about a new Fluffy Bunch character."

The crowd applauded – there was nothing they liked better than a new character. But Gwendolina soon put them straight – this was no ordinary fairy, pony or mermaid. It was time for the Fluffy Bunch Corporation to hear her plan...

"For too long we have relied on the royalties from the Fluffy Bunch characters...

IN THE BIN! I'M GOING TO BUY YOU A **NEW** FLUFFY BUNCH TOY!

MAIN FEATURE: SOFIE the SIMPERING SEA LION

THAT'S ME, FOLKS!

Every time a child bought one of our toys, saw one of our soppy movies or visited Fluffyland our tills rang...

Whenever we've needed to, we've come up with a new character – a bit of pink here, an extra bow there...

THE HORNS FLASH AND PLAY "JINGLE BELLS".

The crowd gasped as Gwendolina, with a swish of her wand, revealed an unspeakable creature...

"It has the tail of a mermaid, the body of a ballerina, the wand of a fairy and the head of puppy," she said proudly. "But best of all, everyone who looks at it will instantly become a Fluffy Lover! **SOON THE ENTIRE WORLD WILL BE A FLUFFY LOVERS' DELIGHT WITH THE FLUFFY BUNCH AS RULERS!!** The Garbage Dump Dummies will be finished for good!"

The crowd applauded.

"Our plans are almost complete," Gwendolina continued. "Now all we need are the tears of laughter of a thousand puppy dogs to give our Creature life."

"But it's almost impossible to make *one* puppy cry with laughter," gasped a pony. "A *thousand*?!"

"I have found a very special 'someone' for the job," gloated Gwendolina. "And soon a Fluffier World will be ours – a world where everyone is Fluffy; a world where the Fluffy Bunch Corporation will rule supreme. **A WORLD WHERE GROSS OUT IS GONE FOR EVER!!**"

10

Unaware of the unfolding Fluffy Bunch plot, Gerald and Gene were sitting alone in the redesigned Gross-Out Den – Fleabag Monkeyface was "training" with the Smugleys.

"Fleabag spends every spare minute with those Smugleys," said Gerald.

"Something's just not right..." said Gene. "We need to investigate."

"But where do we start?" asked Gerald.

"Right here," said Gene. "There's got to be a clue somewhere."

Gerald and Gene started searching the Den for clues. They opened every cupboard and looked behind every Fluffy Bunch toy.

"Fleabag certainly gave this place a spring-clean," said Gerald. "Neatly folded towels, sparkly clean pots and pans..."

"But nothing to tell us why he's stopped being gross," said Gene.

They were just about to give up when Gene thought of one last place to look – the rubbish!

Gerald and Gene never usually went anywhere near Fleabag's rubbish.

But unlike his usual bin, which was so toxic you would have to wear protective clothing to even approach it, everything was placed neatly in labelled boxes.

"There's not a lot we can tell from this stuff," said Gerald. "Apart from the fact that everything Fleabag eats seems to have a Fluffy Bunch logo on it."

Just then something caught Gene's eye – an old cereal box. "Fabby Fairy Flakes breakfast cereal!" he gasped.

"Yes, but there's all kinds of stuff like that in here," said Gerald.

"But I seem to remember him having this box *before* he turned into Fluffpants," said Gene, looking at the bottom of the box. "Yes, I remember him pointing at the sell-by date – he said, 'It's ug-thirty years old. Ug-yum!'"

"You would have thought the ad for that stuff would have put him off," said Gerald.

"Yuck!" choked Gerald. "How can anybody eat that stuff?"

"Well, Fleabag did – all of it, including the free lucky charm, and I'm sure it's got something to do with his strange behaviour," said Gene.

"But how did the box get here in the first place?" asked Gerald.

"I don't know," said Gene. "It's all very strange. First Fleabag goes fluffy then the class gets invited to Fluffyland and now Fleabag is training for the Fluffy Games. And all this started with a box of **Fluffy Bunch cereal**. I think something is going on here."

"The trip to Fluffyland is coming up," said Gerald. "Maybe we'll find out more then."

 It was the day that Gerald and Gene had been dreading and Fleabag couldn't wait for...

"The ug-gates of ug-paradise have ug-opened!" he gushed as they entered Fluffyland. "Let the ug-fun commence!"

"You're free to explore but one area is off limits – the building site," said Mr Troutman, addressing the school party. "They are putting a new attraction in there. We meet at the My Cuddly-Wuddly Pony picnic area for lunch in two hours. Have fun!"

Tickets in hand, Gerald, Gene and the rest of their class were now free to "enjoy" Fluffyland.

As Gerald and Gene had expected, it was the complete opposite of Garbage Dump Dummy World.

THE PINKY THE PINKIEST PIXIE GHOST TRAIN IS ABOUT AS SCARY AS AN ANGRY KITTEN.

Boo!

Unbearably cute Fluffy Bunch characters manned every attraction...

But Fleabag was loving every minute of it!

"Ug-come on, guys, who's going to take a picture of me with ug-Blinky?" he said, posing outside Blinky's Magical Stable. "He is just *sooooo* ug-sparkly!"

OK," said Gerald. "But it's nearly lunchtime. We've got to meet up with Mr Troutman, remember?"

At the My Cuddly-Wuddly Pony picnic area Mr Troutman was waiting.

"All those with packed lunches stay here," he said. "Anyone who would like to have lunch at the Fabby the Fabby-Wabby Wee Fairy Diner, follow me."

As everyone, including Fleabag, was joining Mr Troutman in the diner, Gerald and Gene finally had a chance to have a snoop around.

**12** Meanwhile, in the highest turret of Fluffy Castle, Gwendolina was feeling very pleased with herself.

"Everything is in place exactly as you ordered," said Fifinella. "Fleabag Monkey-thing will be joining us any minute."

"Good, good," murmured Gwendolina. "And the Creature?"

"All he needs are the tears," said Fifinella. "The lagoon is nearly built..."

"Nearly! Nearly?!" screeched Gwendolina. "I don't want to hear 'nearly'... I need it to be ready NOW!"

"I'm afraid it's your new specifications," said Fifinella. "They are taking the builders longer than expected."

"That's not good enough," said Gwendolina. "I want to get the Creature in place and busy making the world *Fluffier* TODAY."

"Well, I was just heading off to speak to the builders," said Fifinella.

"*I'll* go and see the builders," said Gwendolina with her mouth full. "Just as soon as I've finished my cheesy bread."

13

"**W**hat are we looking for?" asked Gerald, as they headed away from the main rides and attractions.

"I'm not sure, but the first place we should check out is that building site," said Gene, pointing at the large boarded-up area covered in "Keep Out" signs. "Something fishy is definitely going on in there."

Gerald and Gene quickly arrived at the site, but the main entrance was heavily guarded by security elves. They could hear diggers and cranes. Frantic work was happening in the forbidden area.

"Looks like this new attraction is going to be huge," said Gerald.

"I'm sure this is connected to what's happened to Fleabag," said Gene. "I don't suppose we'll be invited in. Let's jump the fence."

"Great idea! And look we can put these on," said Gerald, spotting a pair of discarded workman's hard hats.

As quietly as they could Gerald and Gene climbed the fence and were soon inside.

"So many workmen and all they're doing is digging a hole," said Gerald disappointedly.

But before they could explore any further an icy voice echoed across the building site. "Mr Brickman and Mr Digwell, I presume? Fifinella, you told me they were a young, up-and-coming building company, but this is ridiculous."

"I didn't realize they were *that* young," said Fifinella. "But they're meant to be the best in the business."

"It's Gwendolina, Head of the Fluffy Bunch Corporation," whispered Gene. "She seems to think we're the chief builders. Let's play along..."

"Yes," Gene said to Gwendolina, making his voice sound as deep as possible. "We are honoured that you are visiting the site."

"There's no time for small talk," barked Gwendolina. "So my new specifications are holding you up?"

"Er ... we never got any new specifications," said Gene. "What are they?"

"We want the Pink Lagoon to be deeper," said Gwendolina. "Fifinella was meant to tell you. The Creature is even bigger than we first thought."

"Very well," said Gerald, also trying to sound as deep-voiced as possible. "We'll make it deeper."

"And I want more turnstiles," continued Gwendolina. "We expect MILLIONS of visitors here. Because anyone who sees the Creature will want to bring all their friends, and *they* will bring all *their* friends."

"Then they will bring all *their* friends," said Gene, joining in. "Who will bring all *their* friends..."

"Who will then bring *their* friends, who—" said Gerald.

"ENOUGH!" Gwendolina screeched. "When the hairy one's work is done this attraction will be the most popular EVER... EVERYONE who sees it will be turned into a *Lover of All Things Fluffy*... JUST GET THE PINK LAGOON FINISHED BY THE END OF THE DAY!!!"

"Did you say hairy one?" asked Gene.

"Yes, we've got a horrible monkey creature working for us." Gwendolina chuckled. "Fleabag Monkeyface. I recruited him myself. It was a masterstroke. I very nearly surprised myself with my own brilliance! He does everything he's told."

But before Gerald and Gene could find out more, Gwendolina and her entourage about turned and left.

Gerald and Gene were now aware of the impending crisis.

"An attraction that will turn the whole world fluffy?!" gasped Gene. "We've got to stop them!"

"And Fleabag is at the heart of the plot," said Gerald. "But how did Gwendolina recruit him?"

"The box of Fabby Fairy Flakes," said Gene. "She must have planted it in the Gross-Out Den. We need to save Fleabag!"

"And the rest of the world!" added Gerald.

14

But as Gerald and Gene arrived back at the diner, their worst fears were realized – Fleabag was deep in conversation with Mr Troutman and the Smugleys.

"Where have you been?!" barked Mr Troutman when he saw Gerald and Gene. "Fortunately for you this is the proudest day in the school's history: one of our pupils has been invited to participate in the Fluffy Games!"

"There was a last minute cancellation and Fluffpants was asked to fill in," said Randy Smugley.

"Yes," said Mandy. "In fact the first event starts any minute. Goodbye!"

"And good luck!" said Mr Troutman, wiping away a tear. "Why can't you two be more like Fluffpants?"

"We've got to stop them," whispered Gerald.

"Er ... we need to wish Fleabag luck," said Gene as they charged off after Fleabag and his new best friends.

"Just make sure you're on time for the bus back!" called out Mr Troutman.

By the time Gerald and Gene caught up with them, Fleabag and the Smugleys had reached the gates of Fluffy Castle.

"Fleabag! Stop!" cried Gerald. But it was too late – Fleabag and the Smugleys had entered the gates and were heading to the courtyard.

No matter how much Gerald and Gene pleaded there was simply no way they were getting in.

"Only the truly 𝓕𝓵𝓾𝓯𝓯𝔂 are allowed in here," sneered a particularly obnoxious fairy guard. "Just look at you, you probably like Garbage Dump Dummies."

Finally admitting defeat, Gerald and Gene climbed aboard the school bus without Fleabag.

"We *must* save him," said Gene as they returned home.

"But how?" said Gerald. "They are never going to let *us* in."

"We need disguises," said Gene. "And I know just where to get them... But first we need to get these gross-out ingredients together."

Gerald looked at the list.

"What are these for?" he asked.

"I've had an idea," said Gene. "I'll explain later."

15 Meanwhile, back at Fluffy Castle, Gwendolina and her cronies were observing the Fluffy Games from a balcony.

"Everything is in place," said Fifinella. "The fairies are ready, the teacups are ready, Special Agents Randy and Mandy Smugley are ready. All we need is for the Puppy Pageant to start."

"Excellent, excellent," gloated Gwendolina. "And the monkey was the perfect choice for the job."

In the vast courtyard below Fleabag was emerging as the star of the show!

79

"That's the fourth gold medal you've won!" said Randy Smugley. "You're a natural."

"I couldn't have ug-done it without ug-you," said Fleabag. "UG-GROUP HUG!"

Next Up...
Puppy Pageant

After a group hug, Mandy turned to Fleabag. "We must go to the Puppy Pageant," she said, winking at Randy. "They've got over one thousand puppies there!"

"Ug-count me in!" said Fleabag.

As the three of them skipped towards the Pageant, Fleabag had no idea that he was about to take centre stage in the Fluffy Bunch Corporation's dastardly plot!

16 Meanwhile, Gerald and Gene were getting their disguises.

"We need to make ourselves look like lovers of all things fluffy and cuddly," said Gene. "We're going to have to borrow some suitable clothes. And fast!"

First they went to Gene's Auntie Mavis, who owned a fancy-dress shop, to borrow some of her loudest floral shirts.

Then they went to Gerald's Uncle Tom, who used to be a famous actor, to borrow some of his outlandish hats.

And finally they went to school "princess" and general cutie Carleen Petuchi's house to borrow large cuddly toys.

"These outfits make us look ridiculous," said Gerald. "I'm sure I'm getting a rash."

"I know, they're terrible," said Gene. "So have we got all the ingredients for that drink?"

"Old banana peels, slug droppings and some water from the neighbour's dog bowl," replied Gerald.

"Let's put them in a Fluffy Bunch flask," said Gene.

"I've got one here," said Gerald.

"Perfect! Let's get going," said Gene. "Who knows what they are doing to Fleabag now!"

And with that they rushed back to Fluffyland.

17 This time Gerald and Gene had no problem getting past the security guards.

"I told you the outfits would work," whispered Gene.

"Great, but how do we track Fleabag down?" asked Gerald. "This place is huge."

"I guess we just follow the crowd," said Gene.

Everyone was heading in the same direction ...

... to the **Puppy Pageant**.

"This place is making me feel queasy," said Gerald.

"Have you ever seen so many nice clean people in one place," said Gene. "And just look at the puppies!"

Float after float appeared covered in frighteningly cute puppies.

If you're finding this all a bit too fluffy, here is a picture of some maggots having a disco to make you feel better...

Gerald and Gene's horror only increased when they spotted the final float in the procession – at the helm sat none other than Fleabag Monkeyface and his new best friends, Randy and Mandy Smugley.

"We've got to get him away from here," said Gerald. "But how?"

"He seems to be really enjoying himself up there, surrounded by cute puppies. Yuck!" said Gene.

18 In fact being rescued was the last thing on Fleabag's mind because, as Fluffpants Cuddlebug, he was absolutely loving the Pageant. What he didn't realize was that Randy and Mandy were in on the Fluffy Bunch Corporation's plot.

"Oh Fluffpants, wouldn't it be nice to make all these puppies laugh?" said Randy.

"Ug-great idea. Let's get ug-tickling," said Fleabag, grabbing a puppy in a silly hat and tickling it.

"That's cute," said Mandy. "But we need to make *all* the puppies laugh!"

"How can we ug-do that – there's ug-hundreds of them," said Fleabag, still tickling the puppy. "I've only got ug-four hands."

"Perhaps, you could, you know, use some of your **Not-So-Gross-Out Powers**?" wheedled Randy.

"Ug-Not-So-Gross-Out ug-Powers? Ug-yuck!" said Fleabag. "Ug-Fluffpants doesn't want to use ug-horrible ug-Not-So-Gross-Out ug-Powers."

"Pretty please," whined Mandy. "It would be *so* adorable."

"Yes, go on!" said Randy. "It would be the cutest thing ever. Imagine, a *thousand* puppies laughing!"

"Yes, it would be ug-cute," said Fleabag. "Ug-stand back!"

"Go Fluffpants, go Fluffpants!!" chanted Randy and Mandy.

"Ug-time for an ug-turbo tickle!" shouted Fleabag. "Ug-bionic mixed berries and summer fruit belch!"

Fleabag gave a ground-shaking sugary sweet burp and flew into the air before descending in a whirr of turbo-tickling hands...

In a blur of tickling, Fleabag flew through the Pageant,
leaving no puppy untickled.

He tickled puppies
on the left.

He tickled puppies
on the right.

And when his sugary sweet belch ran out of energy, he used bionic nasal candy to juggle a giant dog bone in the air.

This made the puppies laugh even more.

HEE HEE

HEE HEE

HEE HEE

In fact the puppies were laughing so hard they were crying *tears* of laughter!

19

The crowd applauded – they couldn't get enough. But everyone stopped in their tracks when a huge rumbling noise shook the Fluffy Games to the tips of its pink-socked toes.

"Look at that!" said Gerald, pointing at the top of Fluffy Castle.

The highest turret had swung open and a low buzzing noise was coming from it.

"That sounds like bees," said Gene.

Tiny creatures were emerging and flying towards the Pageant.

"Fairies, Gene!" said Gerald. "Thousands of them!"

Each fairy was carrying a small teacup and they were soon buzzing around the puppies.

"They are collecting the puppies' tears," said Gene. "But why?"

Gerald and Gene did not have to wait long to find out because a figure appeared on the balcony of the pink castle.

"Greetings, Oh Fellow Lovers of Fluff, I am Queen Gwendolina, and soon a *Fluffier World* will be ours!"

The crowd applauded.

"Now that we have the tears of laughter of a thousand puppy dogs we can bring you the ultimate Fluffy Bunch character!" she continued. "Please applaud Special Agents Randy and Mandy without whom none of this would have been possible!"

The Smugley twins stepped into the pink castle as the crowd went wild. Fleabag tried to join his new best friends, but was quickly shooed away.

"Your work is done, Monkey-thing," said Gwendolina sternly. "Get away from here!"

"I knew they were in on this," said Gene. "Maybe now Fleabag will see sense."

But Fleabag still had no idea that he had been used by the Fluffy Bunch Corporation and was still in Fluffpants-mode.

"Well done, ug-Randy and ug-Mandy!" he cheered. "To think my ug-best friends are ug-special agents!"

Once again Gwendolina addressed the crowd.

"My Fellow Fluffylovers, come to the Pink Lagoon and see the Creature for yourselves," she purred. "You are about to witness the dawn of a new Fluffy Era... **SOON THE WHOLE WORLD WILL BE FLUFFY!!!**"

20 As the crowd filed out of the courtyard to see the Creature brought to life, Gerald and Gene caught up with Fleabag.

"I ug-love the ug-outfits!" he said. "But what are you ug-doing here?"

"You should have known those horrible Smugleys would betray you in the end," said Gene. "Why don't you come back with us?"

"Ug-betray me? There's been an ug-mix up," said Fleabag. "And I don't want to ug-leave. I ug-like it here. And I ug-like the Smugleys. And ug-puppies. And the ug-Creature from the ug-Pink Lagoon. Let's go and ug-see it!"

"We've got to do something," whispered Gerald. "He's still being Fluffpants."

"That's where the drink comes in," said Gene. "Pass me the flask."

Gene turned to Fleabag. "Oh Fluffpants, after all that tickling and winning medals I think we all need a nice fresh 'n' fluffy fruit juice drink. What do you say?"

"That's an ug-great idea," said Fleabag, cheering up. "And look it's in an ug-Twinkly-Toes the ug-Beautiful Ballet Dancer flask. Ug-lovely!"

Fleabag grabbed the flask and downed the contents in a single gulp. As soon as he swallowed the drink, strange things started happening to him.

"That ... that ug-drink wasn't ug-fresh 'n' fluffy ug-fruit juice," he wailed as his face turned a strange yellow colour. He then began to shake and wobble.

"Duck!" shouted Gerald.

"Ug-banana barf!" screeched Fleabag.

The whole courtyard was covered in a thick yellow gloop. And almost at once Fleabag began to change.

His hair became messy and nits started to reappear...

His neat sports vest became covered in goo...

And most reassuringly of all, his nose started to run...

"Ug-gross!" said Fleabag, before a huge grin spread across his hairy face. "But I ug-like it!"

The old Fleabag was back!

"We missed you!" said Gerald and Gene.

Just then Gene spotted something out of the corner of his eye.

"Just as I suspected, a Lucky Fabby Fairy Charm,"
he said, scooping up a small pink object shaped like
a fairy. "I knew it – Gwendolina made Fleabag fluffy
by planting a box of thirty-year-old Fabby Fairy Flakes
in the Gross-Out Den!"

"She knew Fleabag would eat the lot," said Gerald.

"Including the charm. It must contain some kind of
fluff poison," said Gene, sealing it in a plastic bag. "And
it looks like it would still work – it's twinkling."

"That was ug-in my ug-stomach all along?" said
Fleabag. "Yuck!"

"Well, it's out now," said Gerald. "We don't need
to meet Fluffpants Cuddlebug again ... ever!"

"We've got to stop them bringing the Creature to life," said Gene.

But before they could move they were surrounded by fairy guards. The yellow gloop had ruined Gerald and Gene's disguises and it was clear that Fleabag was no longer Fluffpants.

"You must leave Fluffyland at once," barked a fairy. "Gwendolina has given strict instructions that you three are to be ejected on sight!"

And with that Gerald, Gene and Fleabag were bundled out through a back door.

21 But, inside, Fluffyland was a hive of activity. "Congratulations, Special Agents Randy and Mandy," cooed Gwendolina. "You shall be rewarded. Fifinella is already working on **Randy and Mandy Smugley dolls**. You will be immortalized as Fluffy Bunch characters for ever!"

"Thank you, Your Majestic Marvellousness," said Randy. "We were only too pleased to be of service."

"The hardest part was hanging around with that ... that thing." Mandy grimaced. "He may have gone fluffy but he was still a disgusting monkey creature."

"Well, his sort will soon be a thing of the past," said Gwendolina. "Now let us hurry. We must bring our Creature to life."

Gwendolina and her party made their way to a large platform overlooking the Pink Lagoon. Inside the Creature lay dormant.

"If my calculations are right, the Creature should come to life as soon as the puppies' tears are added!" said Gwendolina. "Decant the precious liquid!"

One by one the fairies deposited the contents of their teacups into the pool.

There was a twitching ... then a stretching ... and the Creature sprang to life! It was so fluffy a powerful glow beamed from its face. A glow that would turn all who looked at it into a *Fluffy Lover*.

"The Creature ... it's ... it's ALIVE!" cried Gwendolina. "The tears worked. My plan is truly a thing of sparkling beauty!!! Now, open the gates. **LET'S START TURNING THE WORLD FLUFFY!!!**"

22 As people flocked to see the new attraction, Gerald, Gene and Fleabag tried to work out a way to stop the impending flufftastrophe. But with the huge crowd jostling shoulder to shoulder there was no way in.

"There's only one thing for it," said Gene. "We're going to have to use **Gross-Out Power**!"

"With ug-pleasure," said Fleabag, who couldn't wait to get his own back on the horrible Smugley twins and their queen.

BRAND-NEW ATTRACTION!!!
The Creature from the Pink Lagoon!

As Fleabag began to attack the huge walls with earwax pellets, it didn't take long for some familiar figures to appear on the ramparts above.

"What are *you* still doing here? Do you really think you can take on the Fluffy Bunch Corporation and win?" said Gwendolina. "Unleash the Weapons of Mass Fluffstruction."

Randy and Mandy wheeled out a terrifying device.

"Behold the Fluff-terminator!" said Gwendolina. "Now, FIRE!"

"I don't like the look of that," said Gerald.

"Duck!" shouted Gene. They were being bombarded with thousands of cuddly toys, dolls and fairy cakes!

"I'll ug-get them!" said Fleabag.

But under the constant barrage of fluffy objects pelting down on them, Fleabag could not get close enough to use any of his Gross-Out Powers.

"We need to get out of here!" said Gerald.

"See how they flee!" crowed Gwendolina.

"Give in to the *Power of Fluff*!" called out Randy.

"You know you want to!" added Mandy.

"Never!" replied Gene, as they retreated from Fluffyland. "We'll be back!"

23 Over the next few days, Gerald, Gene and Fleabag desperately tried to come up with a plan as crowds thronged into Fluffyland. Finally Gene had an idea.

"Follow me," he said. "There is one person who can help us – Samuelson Stinx!"

But when they got to Garbage Dump Dummy World the place was deserted.

"This place is ug-great!" said Fleabag, who now appreciated the world's grossest theme park.

"Yes, but where are all the **Lovers of Gross Out**?" wondered Gerald.

"I thought this place would be really busy," said Gene. "Let's find Mr Stinx."

Gerald, Gene and Fleabag finally tracked down Samuelson Stinx in his workshop.

"Word is spreading about the new attraction at Fluffyland." Mr Stink sighed. "All my visitors are cancelling and going there."

"The Creature is already having an effect," said Gerald. "We need to stop it!"

"But how?" asked Mr Stinx. "Fluffyland has the best security in the business, and if we so much as look at the Creature we're done for."

"I have an idea," said Gene. "But it will require something from your workshop, at the back where you keep the fluffy prototypes."

"Anything you like," said Mr Stinx.

Gerald, Fleabag and Mr Stinx all looked confused. But Gene was about to explain his idea.

"Very well," said Mr Stinx, as they reached the back of the workshop. "But what could be of use here?"

"The belching bunny," said Gene. "You've heard the story of the Trojan horse? Mr Troutman told us about it in class."

"The one where an army hid inside a giant wooden horse to sneak into the city of Troy?" said Gerald. "The people in the castle brought it in then the army jumped out and surprised them."

"Exactly," said Gene. "Well, to get into Fluffyland we're going to need a **Trojan Bunny**. And, Mr Stinx, you're going to customise it for us. We'll need it to hop!"

 **24** Meanwhile, strange things were starting to happen all over town. And from the highest turret of Fluffy Castle, Gwendolina was loving every minute of it...

"The Creature is already having an impact," said Fifinella.

"Excellent, excellent," said Gwendolina. "And this is just the beginning. Soon the whole world will be fluffy and no one can stop us!"

"The Bunny is now ready!" announced an exhausted Mr Stinx. "I'll just grab some **Garbage Dump Dummy Stink Powder** for the Lagoon. It turns even the cleanest, purest liquids into putrid gloop."

"Great!" said Gene. "Let's go!"

With everyone on board Mr Stinx fired up the engine. The bunny chugged into life and, although it felt quite unstable, it seemed to be working.

"To Fluffyland!" said Gene.

"To Fluffyland!" said Gerald, Fleabag and Mr Stinx.

HOPPITY HOP-HOP

But what was going on at the gates of Fluffyland almost made the bunny topple over.

People emerging from the theme park were behaving in the most frighteningly fluffy ways – some were dancing, some were singing corny songs, some were picking flowers ... and everywhere there was unnecessary group-hugging going on.

"Look at these people," said Gerald. "They must have seen the Creature from the Pink Lagoon. The world is going fluffy!"

"Gwendolina's plan is working!" said Gene. "Just look at the queue!"

Thousands of people desperate for a glimpse of the legendary new Fluffy Bunch character waited in a line that stretched round the block and out of sight.

Mr Stinx carefully parked the giant Bunny outside the main entrance to Fluffyland.

"Now it's a waiting game," said Gene. "Let's hope they go for it."

As the day drew to a close, the crowds finally lessened. It was night-time and all was quiet.

"They must have noticed it by now," said Gerald.

And sure enough, outside the Trojan Bunny they could hear voices ... fairy voices!

They were finally being wheeled into Fluffyland.
The plan was working!

"Just wait until Gwendolina sees this!" said one of
the fairy security guards. "She's going to love it!"

After a while the Bunny came to a stop. They were
right in the heart of Fluffyland.

26 It was time for them to get to work.

"Let's move the Bunny as close to the Pink Lagoon as possible," said Mr Stinx.

But as they hopped along, Mr Stinx failed to notice an open gate outside Blinky the Sparkliest Unicorn's Magical Stable. As the Trojan Bunny hit the door, there was a familiar clicking noise.

"Oh dear," said Mr Stinx as the robotic bunny voice started to boom out.

"2 ... 1..."

"I thought I'd disconnected the belching mechanism!" said Mr Stinx.

"What happened to 5, 4 and 3?!" said Gene.

There was no time for Fleabag to use his Gross-Out Powers this time and the Bunny let off a theme-park-shaking belch!

Powerful lights shone out and security fairies were suddenly everywhere – and leading them, in her pyjamas, was Gwendolina herself!

"We should never have allowed that Bunny in here!" she screeched. "I *knew* it was a trap!"

"The game's up, Gwendolina," said Mr Stinx, trying to sound as confident as possible.

"Well, if it isn't **Pinkyson Pinx**," said Gwendolina, recognizing her former employee.

"*Pinkyson Pinx.*" Gene chuckled. "What kind of a name is that?"

"I had to change my name to something fluffy to get the job," said Samuelson Stinx.

"Enough chatter!" boomed Gwendolina. "It is time to make **YOU** Fluffy. Unveil the Creature!"

The fence in front of the Pink Lagoon started to lower – they were about to be exposed to the Creature from the Pink Lagoon ... and turned into Fluffy Lovers!

"Gross-Out Goggles!" said Gene. "Good thing we brought these along. Put them on quickly!"

With their goggles on the Creature didn't look fluffy at all. In fact it looked like a disgusting blob.

"Cool!" said Gerald.

"Unreal!" said Gene.

"Ug-brilliant!" said Fleabag.

"They work!" said Mr Stinx.

The Gross-Out Goggles were doing their job – the Creature's powers weren't working on them.

"What's going on?" hissed Gwendolina. "Why aren't they turning in to Fluffy Lovers? Guards, get them! Time to send this lot to the tickling cell!"

"Tickling cell?" said Gerald. "I don't like the sound of that!"

"We're trapped!" said Mr Stinx. "We need to get the **Stink Powder** into that Lagoon. It's our only hope of counteracting the puppy tears!"

"Yes," said Gerald. "But we're completely surrounded."

27

"Time for some Gross-Out Power, Fleabag," said Gene. "You've got to get to that Lagoon."

Fleabag grabbed the bag of Stink Powder. "Ug-turbo sneeze!" he said, jumping over the guards.

Fleabag was now right above the Lagoon.

"Release the powder!" shouted Gene.

As Fleabag sprinkled it over the pool, the water started to fizz and boil. The colour changed from pink to murky green.

"It's working!" said Mr Stinx. "Soon the Creature will love all things gross!"

"What have you done to my Creature?" bleated Gwendolina. "Unleash the **Fairies of Doom**!"

Once again there was a loud buzzing noise as thousands of fairies appeared from the highest turret. But this time they were not carrying teacups and they were looking distinctly angry.

"My ug-Gross-Out Power can't ug-hold them back!" said Fleabag as he tried to ward off the micro-peril.

"We're doomed!" wailed Mr Stinx. Then all of a sudden a large splat of green gloop landed on Gwendolina. Then another, and another.

"What is this stuff!" winced the Fairy Queen. "It's ... it's disgusting!"

"The Creature!" cried Gene. "It's firing at everything Fluffy ... including the Smugleys!"

Pretty soon the whole of Fluffyland and all the fairies were covered in a green gloopy substance. Gwendolina was now begging for the Creature to stop! **GROSS OUT HAD SAVED THE DAY!!!**

"All my fluffy work, ruined, RUINED, RUINED!" cried Gwendolina.

She made a final bid to get to the Fluff-terminator but the Creature was too quick for her. Finally drenched in gloop from the tip of her wand to the top of her Fairy Queen crown, Gwendolina begged for mercy. "Make the Creature stop – I'll do anything!"

28 A few weeks later Gerald, Gene and Fleabag were back at Garbage Dump Dummy World to film the opening of a brand-new attraction.

"In the end I agreed to take the Creature away." Mr Stinx chuckled. "Bookings have skyrocketed!"

"So what about Gwendolina?" asked Gerald. "Last time we saw her she was up to her neck in green gloop."

"She was only allowed to wash it off *after* she had promised never to try and make the world Fluffy again," said Mr Stinx. "There's room for Fluffy *and* Gross out there!"

The Creature from the Gross Lagoon

"Yes, and we're getting it all on film!" said Gene.

"Ug-brilliant!" said Fleabag, getting in position to present Gross-Out TV's first-ever programme.

But just as they started filming there was a loud splashing noise. The **Creature** spat a blob of gloop in the air and it landed right on the camera!

"Ruined!" said Gene. "When are we *ever* going to make a film?"

"I'll buy you a new camera," said Mr Stinx. "Without you I'd have gone bust."

When Gerald, Gene and Fleabag got back to the Gross-Out Den they had definitely had enough of theme parks.

"This place stinks!" Gerald winced. "It's great to have it back to normal!"

"No more Fluffy," said Gene. "And no more Fluffpants!"

"Ug-brilliant!" said Fleabag, placing a set of Garbage Dump Dummies on the mantelpiece.

But then a strange light started glowing outside.

"What now?" Gene chuckled. "Aliens?"

To find out more, read the next "Disgusting Adventure of Fleabag Monkeyface" – which makes this one seem like the kind of book you would take home to read to your parents. **Don't say we didn't warn you!!!**

If you can't wait until the next
Fleabag Monkeyface book, here's
a free comic to keep you going.
(It makes perfect on-the-toilet reading!)